WHO KILLED PRANEETA

MOHD JUNAID

ISBN 978-93-5458-904-1
© MOHD JUNAID 2021
Published in India 2021 by Pencil

Contributors:
Co-Author: Nikhil C.

A brand of
One Point Six Technologies Pvt. Ltd.
123, Building J2, Shram Seva Premises,
Wadala Truck Terminal, Wadala (E)
Mumbai 400037, Maharashtra, INDIA
E connect@thepencilapp.com
W www.thepencilapp.com

Author biography

Mohd junaid, aged twenty six, junaid has been trying to write this book for 2 years.Junaid has also directed in short films and also writes the story of short films screen paly. This is his first novel.

CONTENTS

Chapter One 7

Acknowledgements

This is the work of fiction. Any resemblance to people, living or dead, or events is purely coincidental.

First of all, I want to thank each and every reader who is going to make my story alive by living in it through the pages of this book. I feel immensely blessed to reach out to the readers through this book and will love to give all of them a huge credit as you must know, just like I am the creator of this nook, 'you' are the creator of the 'writer' in me, 'you' are the purpose of why I wrote this book and 'you' are the one to give my story a life by reading it. So, a big thumbs up for you.

Well, now I will like to take the names without whom it wouldn't have been possible to write this book. I am and will always be thankful to my brother and sister who always believed in me and encouraged me choose the path of my wish. They are the reason why Idared to believe in myself and my dreams.

I want to thank my closest friends for cheering me up on my way to complete this book.

Thank 'you' once again! Cheers!

Chapter One

PRESENT DAY.

HOTEL PLAZA ROOM - NIGHT

The shower of the hotel room is on, AJJU (film producer) is Taking bath, suddenly someone knock the door of the AJJUS'S room badly. If Ajju takes a few seconds more to open the door then person breaks the door because he is very angry. suddenly he stopped knocking on the door... when Ajju slowly opened the door, then suddenly the unknown person came back and inter in the room.

AJJU begs the person for his life, but he does not listen to him and kills him with a sharp knife. "No leave me...Let me go. What do you want...I will give you a lot of money...Let me go please?"

###

News channel on television- morning. News reader (Female 25Y) on television reading news. "It has been reported that the famous Bollywood film producer Ajju was brutally murdered by someone by entering the hotel room last night. Police is probing the matter but the culprit has not been found yet."

The next day, police team arrive at the crime scene to find out who the killer is?

ACP Raman Singh, "Got any clues to the murder? any marks? Who came yesterday to meet him and check all the cameras of the hotels? Send the body for post-mortem."

"Sir we checked the camera but nothing was found and yesterday don't disturb was tagged at the door of the room." When the room service person came in the morning, he opened the door with his card and got scared seeing the dead body and informed the manager." SAB Inspector Chetan Mane replied.

ACP Raman Singh, "Call him... get information from him. Maybe he knows something..." Find out who was staying in a nearby room. Maybe they have heard something.

ACP RAMAN SINGH looks at the dead body ...... speaks in a slow voice while thinking.

"Find out with whom it was last night. was there someone" ACP Raman Singh Said.

Ok sir....

###

FEW DAYS AGO........DELHI- INDIA.......

Ambulance stopped at Praneeta's house Delhi Two men descend from an ambulance with a dead body.it is raining heavily. They go inside the house carrying the dead body. Seeing the dead body, Praneeta's mother starts screaming a lot.

Mom, "Pari…. Pari, open your eyes, talking to me, say something, why are you silent? say something, your father is no longer angry with you. Now say something. Pari. Won't you talk to your mother?

Yash enters home running away. And due to rain, it slips down…. Seeing the body of Praneeta, his eyes are filled with tears. Mother comes running to Yash and say,

"See Yash. Praneeta is not saying anything. You tell it to talk to me. Won't you talk to your mother? Why is it silent? Say something son."

"Please mother take care of yourself" Then Yash puts his hand on his father's shoulder…

Dad, "How do I take care of myself? I had refused, was also stopped, do you know what

is the biggest sorrow in life? Shoulder the funeral of a young daughter.

I had a dream. I will send my beloved daughter away from home after marrying like princesses. O my god! Why keep me alive to see this day? would have killed me, I want to die now.

###

Some people are sitting around praneeta's dead body, "Whatever is happening in the world, there is Gods will in it, no one can stop it. Our live and die is already fixed… Yash is also sitting there. And he is crying.

Yash is remembering all those things of Praneeta.

Yash is sitting in the courtyard of his house and remembers Pranitha's childish antics.

"How do you start a fight with any such goons? Yash Said.

"As long as you are with me, no one can harm me."

YASH, "Hey...this is not a film where the hero kills many at the same time...isn't it"

I know you are fattu...You will not help me if someone teases or troubles me? Praneeta said.

"Far from teasing, even if someone lifts his eyes and sees, I will break his eyes."

While speaking, Yash hug Praneeta...

All the people are in the cremation ground and Yash gives **fire** to Praneeta's dead body.

Note:*Pitrumedha or Antyakarma or Antyeshti or cremation is the sixteenth rites of the Hindu religion. After death, this rite performed by the recitation of Veda mantras are also called cremation, cremation and funeral rituals etc. In this, the dead body is ritually dedicated to the fire after death. Both manual bamboo wood pyres and electric cremation are used for Hindu cremations. For the latter, the body is kept on a bamboo frame on rails near the door of the electric chamber. After cremation, the mourner will collect the ashes and consecrate it to a water body, such as a river or sea.*

###

Yash is sleeping and saw a dream.... some boys are following to Praneeta and he grabs Praneetas hand...

SLUM BOY, "Hey what's wrong with us? We belong to your family. Look how many people we have. All of them have sister-in-law, you and my life...."

"Have you seen your face in the mirror" Praneeta said.

"I see my face every day. Now you are not a Katrina or Deepika...who will get a hero to love you...then you will have to love me only."

"Leave my hand, let me go, Otherwise, I will injure you with my leg in such a place, the whole life will stand in front of the mirror and dance."

Slum Boy, "Hey...look... your sister-in-law's blood is very hot...she speaks as the fire is coming out. Listen, this is your arrogance...you reduce it a little bit. Otherwise, it will cost you dearly. I will make you in such a condition that your face will not be worth showing."

"Get out of my way." Praneeta said.

"Otherwise, what would you do"

Praneeta, she says with full fervour, I don't ... he will...You look behind you

Yash is stand behind them. they turned and shocked. The boy gets scared after seeing Yash.

Slum Boy, (Speaks fearfully) Who are you? Go away from here. here is the question of my life... I can't kill you in front of a piece of my moon more precious than my life.

Yash, "You have made a big mistake by calling my sister a piece of the moon. And after today your life will never get stuck in questions."

"Will you beat me" Slum boy said.

Yash speaks with an angry face, you heard it wrong... I will not only beat you... I will kill you all.

Hearing this, the slum boy gets very angry and then he asks one of his boys to bring Yash to him while beating Yash.

"Catch him....and dragging it and putting it on my feet."

And then a man comes forward and Yash beating by flying kick and on boy Falls down on the ground. There is a lot of conflict in everyone after few minutes the slums boys begs for his life.

"Brother, leave me. I have made a big mistake" slums boys said.

But YASH does not leave anybody kills everyone badly. And in the last, Yash kills the slums boy. During this, a lot of injury to Yash.

Praneeta ties bandage on Yash's hand.

Yash, "Why take such troubles...? Whose results are like this...?

"You can't even protect your sister" Praneeta Replied.

Yash, "Till when? After all, one day you will get married and go away from this house... very far from me."

"Will our relationship end if we go away? If I ever have a problem, won't you help me" Praneeta said.

Yash, "I will kill whoever gives you problems"

"Otherwise, what is the use of tying **Rakhi** to you when you can't protect your sister" .... Praneeta said.

Note: Rakhi Meaning "safety" and "bond", Raksha Bandhan celebrates the unique bond between a brother and his sister. The festival is observed on the full-moon day or Purnima in the Hindu calendar month of Shravan.

Suddenly he (Yash) opens his eyes and said...

Yash, "I find out your killer... and the same will happen to him as he did to you."

###

Yash travelling in flight from Delhi to Mumbai..Yash is in the Delhi airport and talks to his friend Shubham on the phone call.

Hello! Shubham.... Send me the address...

"Ok. i send you. call me after you reach Mumbai." Shubham said.

"Ok...I do."

###

Taxi is stopped at address given by Shubham....Yash has paid his bill and start walk-in in building. At the window Asmita is watching him....and she is very excited.

Asmita, "She says these words with smile and slowly voice" Ooh hoo .... what a boy...you are gone now, In my love...

Asmita open her room door and she said...

Hi! I am Asmita…your neighbour….

"Hi." Yash replied.

Yash does not pay much attention to Ashmita and goes to his room... Yash lock the door...

Asmita, "Attitude, so much Attitude...One day you will yearn to get love from this Ashu.

She said this word in a low voice...and return to her room and close the door.

###

Yash is going to Praneeta's house. Car is stopped at building. And he went to her floor. And room is locked... because This is the place where Praneeta's murder took place.... He watched left and right and open the door. slowly slowly...he entered in the room. And searching some things...

"Pari, what is this place? how can I find your murderer...? something like this...to find out? He said this word in a low voice....

And suddenly Yash's phone is ringing. And he receives the call.

"Dad did you get Praneeta's mobile......?"

"No....what happened Yash.? are you fine?" Yash's father replied on phone call.

"Yes Dad! I am fine...but now he will not be fine...who has killed my sister."

"Whatever you do, son. before that think about us too, that your mother and your father are also there... We have lost Praneeta. If something like this happens to you too...we will die like this too...Yash."

"Yes dad. I will call you back...bye...take care of yourself..."

After the call is disconnected, Yash starts searching for Pranitha's phone...Yash gets Pranitha's mobile phone at the bottom of the bed.... Yash keeps the phone in his pocket and goes towards his house...

Yash called to Shubham and share Praneeta's phone number for Trace the all-call details....

"I am sharing a mobile number with you. want call details of last two month."

"It's a bit difficult...but I try." Shubham replied.

Yash gets angry after hearing Shubham.

"Don't say bit difficult. I want details if I want..."

"OK. I will try...but it will take some time."

"You just give me these details…"

"Whose number is this?" Shubham asked.

"What will do?"

"Tell me, whose number is this?"

"You will know whose number it is then you will not do my work"

Shubham, "tell me"

"My sister Praneeta's mobile number is..."

"Who has been murdered?" Shubham asked.

"Yes" Yash replied.

Shubham scared to hear this...and said, "I can't do this. if something goes wrong, my career will be ruined. You are asking to get the call details of such a person's number. which is not even in this world..."

Yash, "She came in my dream...she told me that I will protect her, always. He said wherever I live, stay in any condition, Protect me. So now I know that if someone has murdered her then, how can I sit and watch silently? Whoever did this will have to pay the price..."

"I will try to find out...but my name should not come in all this." Shubham replied.

###

A FEW MONTHS BEFORE PRANEETA'S MURDER*****

Praneeta is auditioning in studio, "Hi! my name is Praneeta, I am 25-year-old height 5.5 inches." And then she started her dialogue, *"Why did you come in my life? Everything was going well. there was no tension. oh my God! What should I do now, when you could not be my own then why come to me? You got what you wanted, then left me...?"*

When Praneeta finished her audition, the camera man said, "Very good. You will be called for next round."

"Why not get a film with Shahrukh or Salman Khan?" Praneeta asked.

"Madam, if the director / producer likes your acting, then you will be called."

"Yes... I know, I'm not going to get a call."

###

Outside the studio, Pranitha checked the phone. Nisha's 14 missed calls on Praneeta's phone. Praneeta calls Nisha.

PRANEETA, Hello! Nisha, where are you?

"Why was the call not received?" Nisha asked.

"Yes. I saw 14 missed calls... I came to audition today... you tell why so many calls...?

"Sunny's call came to me; tomorrow is a party. And there are film producers / business men and people from some political parties are also going to come. Let me introduce you to Sunny." Nisha said.

"Ok. you send me the address and i will meet you tomorrow."

Nisha, "Ok bye."

Praneeta, "take care."

\#\#\#

PRANEETA'S MUMBAI HOME – NIGHT

Praneeta is talking to her mother on video call...Praneeta on phone.

"Hello! Mom, how are you...?"

"I'm fine, how are you, how are you doing?" Mom replied.

"I am fine too. Just miss you all a lot"

"Praneeta! My angel daughter, I am saying that you come back home. In our family, girls don't do jobs... but you have gone to Mumbai... It's an unknown city. I care a lot about you." Mom said.

"No mom, I can't come back now. How's dad? Is he still angry with me?"

"His anger is justified Praneeta. how can a father let his daughter go alone in an unknown city? You ask yourself and see... he asks about you every day."

Praneeta, "sorry mom. please don't force me. When I left the house. I only thought that whatever I am going to do today papa will be very angry, but one day they will be proud of me... And how many days can I be angry with his dear daughter. when they did not want to, I will fly, then why do he call me Pari (Fairy)?"

"Your dad lovingly named you Praneeta." Mom replied.

"And I made this name my passion."

"Hmmm." Mom said.

"Mom, how is Yash?" Praneeta said.

"That's fine too."

Praneeta, "ok mom take care of yourself. I will talk to you later."

"Ok! Praneeta... take care of yourself too..." Mom said.

###

NEXT DAY_ NIGHTCLUB

Nisha makes a phone call to Praneeta. Then a cab stops in front of Nisha...Praneeta gets down from the cab...

Nisha, "Where were you...? How long have I been waiting for...? why late? The phone is not reachable ... Do you know what a big party this is? So why are you so late?"

"Do you know the traffic of Mumbai? Let's go to the party inside." Praneeta replied.

They Enter in the night club, there are lots of people present. Some are dancing, some are drinking, some are flirting around with the girls. Then Nisha's eyes fall on Sunny and she told to Praneeta.

"Look she is Sunny... let me introduce you to her"

"Ok! Let's go"

Nisha, "Hi! Sunny...how are you? Meet my friend Praneeta."

"Hi! Beautiful ladies! Sunny said. And Sunny kissed Pranitha's hand. "Where are you from, Praneeta?"

Praneeta slowly releases her hand and reply.

"New Delhi"

"OK... so how did you come to Mumbai?" Sunny asked.

"Madam want to be an actress.... wants to act in films." Nisha said.

"OK. have you worked in any film or in any songs?" Sunny asked.

Praneeta said, "No"

"Since her childhood, she wants to work in films after watching the films." Nisha said.

"So what? I want to become an actress, and definitely one day I will be become an actress." Praneeta replied.

"Do you have any identity in this industry?" Sunny asked"

If it had any Link, she wouldn't have been here.... would have appeared in a film with Shah Rukh Khan or Salman." Nisha replied.

Sunny said, "See how it is for those who are beginners, it is very difficult for them to get work in films, even if got a small role in films...and to get a big role some big work has to be done. Are you understanding? what am I talking about?"

Sunny turns his hand in Praneeta's hair....

Praneeta (Nervousness voice) "I'm sorry ...I don't understand what you are saying."

"Hey, Nisha tell her it's not that easy." Sunny said.

Nisha, "What a bastard you are?"

"Nisha, you know that naivety does not work here... if you want to do something, you have to be shameless." Sunny explained.

"Nisha let's go from here. I will make my arrangements." Praneeta said.

Hey! you will not be able to do anything...Here is my many Acquaintances, look at the Gaye, he is a producer, he is standing here, if you say yes then can I talk to him for you?"

"Nisha, let's go from here. I do not want the favour of such people, those who only want to use girls... A man who cannot respect a woman, what work will he give to her?" Praneeta said.

Sunny, "Yes can you go...and if you get work easily then tell me too.... I will also come to work in the film."

Praneeta leaves from there…

###

Nisha and Pranitha are sitting in the cab, Praneeta is very angry.

"Praneeta, "What nonsense does he talk…. what does he understand himself"?

"He is right too. Praneeta think once and see… who are you…? Nisha said.

"What do you mean? Am I not beautiful...? Is my height short? Or is my figure bad?"

"No, there is no bad things in you, just you are not the daughter of any film star or any producer, which you can easily get work in the film."

"So, what should I do." Praneeta asked.

"You know what you have to do…. so, think and do."

"I will not do this…. I'm sorry." Praneeta replied.

Praneeta asked to stop the cab...

"Stop the car…. I have to get out of this car." Cab is stop, Praneeta gets down from the cab...

###

AFTER FEW DAYS OF PRANEETA'S MURDER
****

YASH'S HOME – MORNING - MUMBAI

The milk man was knocking on the door and YASH was sleeping in the room .... Then suddenly he opens his eyes.... At the door, a milk man (little boy)) was standing.

Yash, "told you how many times, not to ring the bell away. Put the packet in silence and go away."

"It should be known my money is safe or not, tomorrow you got up and told me that, "you have not taken milk", then who will be charged for my money, right?"

Yash picks up a packet of milk in his hand and close the door of the room......

Yash's phone is ringing, Shubham who's Yash's friend gets Praneeta's call details but ask Yash to promise him that no one should come to know that I gave the details to you. Yash's assures Shubham that he will keep this secret.

"Hi! Yash, I have sent all the call details of Praneeta to your phone, check it."

"OK"

And Yash dial the last number but no one answer the call.

###

Yash goes to a nightclub, on song track, Yash asks for a whiskey from the waiter.

"One Whiskey please."

Yash saw a girl dancing in the club. The girl is scared of seeing Yash. She tries to hide from YASH, Yash seeing girl is hiding, he goes towards, and starts chasing her. Seeing Yash coming towards her, the girl gets scared and starts running away to the exit...

The girl is running and she goes to the car parking lot. Yash follows her in the parking lot. Then the sound of a car begins to sound.... Yash try to reach the car. But the speed of the car is very high, And the car gets out of parking.

Yash is thinking, "why was the girl looking at me and why she running? Maybe she knows something about my sister... Or has She killed my sister?"

###

PARKING LOT-T.V. NEWS CHANNEL

A security guard is sitting in the parking lot watching the news in TV. There is a television in the parking lot where the news reader reads the news.

"In view of the increasing number of murders in Mumbai, women are scared to leave the house late at night. Now there have been more than 5 murders. but the police have not been able to trace the murderer yet. Should we consider it a defeat of the police or negligence?? All the blood that has been done so far has been killed mercilessly. From this it seems that the police do not care about the public." Yash sees the security guard and leaves the parking place....

###

YASH'S HOME - NIGHT

Yash is trying to Praneeta's turn mobile phone on... And suddenly Phone turns on...The unread massages suddenly started coming on Praneeta's phone...ONE massage received on Praneetas phone, in which it was written that. "Hi! Praneeta 25000k transfer in your bank account...see you in the party Tomorrow at Sunny's farm house .... I am sending you the address.... then Yash calls that number but that number is not reachable...Yash thinks that, "once he goes to that address to find out who send the message and for which purpose, and why he or she gave the money".

###

GIVEN ADDRESS IN SMS-FARMHOUSE-NIGHT

Yash gets out of his car and then he enters the farm house... There are lots of people there... Some people are dancing... And some people are having fun with girls... Some have been drunk.... Yash trying to finds the person who sent the message on the PRANEETA's phone...

Yash's eye falls on a girl who was dancing in the nightclub that night and then the girl saw Yash then she ran from that place. YASH calls the number from which the message came from, ... When the call is connected, the phone rings ring the phone of Nisha who had been in a nightclub that night...Nisha is nervous by seeing Yash calling on her phone. Then she tries to hide from YASH.... this time Yash catches her.

###

OUTSIDE THE FARMHOUSE- NIGHT-

Yash gets down from the car and Nisha gets out of the car's Diggy. Nisha tries to run away but Yash catches her....

"Leave me please."

"Who are you... and why do you run after seeing me"

"When I saw you for the first time, I was scared... that's why I ran." Nisha said.

"Why did you send money to Praneeta... do you know where Praneeta is...?"

"No"

"She has been murdered... because of you... because of you who do this dirty work."

Nisha gets scared after hearing this. And she sit-down and start crying.

"Why did you send money to Praneeta?"

"We go to the party... which is attended by the rich people of the city. Producer. Film director. Business man. Praneeta thought that she would get work. So, she used to go to these parties."

"Because of all your fault, Praneeta has been murdered."

Yash is very angry and he now slap Nisha.

"Let me go I don't know anything about her murder please. I don't know anything...."

Nisha is crying...

"She used to disappear like this for a few days without telling... then suddenly she used to come back... and didn't even tell me anything." Please leave me…please.

"No not like this, you have made such a big mistake. You should be punished for it." Yash said.

"Please let me go.... please. Please..."

Even after a lot of begging with Yash, Yash does not let her go. YASH put guns on Nisha's head... Seeing this, Nisha is scared... And she starts crying....

"You will die now... you will have to die."

"No! please, I didn't do anything, I just wanted to help her, and with whom she used to go, and where she used to go, Sunny knows all these things. please let me go."

"Where will this Sunny be found...?" Yash asked.

"Sunny lives in Goa. He does all his work from there. Every Sunday he comes to Mumbai, you ask him. He would know." Nisha said.

"Where does he come to Mumbai?" Yash asked.

"The place is not fixed... He informs me when he comes."

Yash said, "Do you have any photo of him?"

Nisha, "Yes, it is in my phone."

Nisha has sent Sunny's photo to Yash. Yash leaves Nisha and goes away...

###

AFTER TWO DAYS……

Yash is driving a car and his phone rings; Nisha's call has come.

Nisha on call, "Sunny is coming to Mumbai today."

"Where? and send me the address." Yash replied.

Nisha, "Yes. I send you now."

Then she sends the address to Yash on his phone.

###

NIGHTCLUB - NIGHT

Yash goes to the pub and looks for Sunny. On seeing Sunny, he runs and goes to him. There is a great confrontation between the two.

Yash is surrounded by the 8 gunmen. The lead goes for his gun...and is disabled by an elbow to the face. Yash then double taps the 2 gunmen, and dodges a spray from an SMG, which riddles the disabled gunman. Yash charges forward, and double taps tow gunman-FOUR left...

Yash ducks behind a pillar calmly ejects the clip. A gunman comes around the corner, but is disabled by a strike to the throat Yash reloads, and double taps.

YAHS tosses the body one way, the gunman sprays the diversion, and Yash emerges from the other side. With each step he double taps, one down, tow down, tow left.

Yash then fights with the other two, tosses one over his back, and double taps the other. Finishes the last gunman off.

Sunny tries to escape but Yash comes down a stair when.... he is ambushed by Sunny, who pulls a gun, and shoots Yash in his shoulder, but Yash slams the gun into the wall.

Sunny dashes through a set of double doors, and is tackled by Sunny, who sticks Yash's wounded shoulder, one. Twice...the two blows until YASH gets SUNNY in a headlock with his legs.

Sunny said, "why do you want to kill me? what have I done to you?"

Yash is very angry...

"You are a murderer, you have killed." Yash explained.

"Whom have I murdered?" Sunny asked.

"You have killed my sister Praneeta ... and now you will have to pay the price for it."

There is a lot of fight between the two.

Sunny said, "I didn't kill her... I sent Praneeta with Rocky... After that she didn't talk to me, she hid somewhere and she has my drugs too."

Yash breaks Sunny's neck. Yash is also injured; he is shot by Sunny. Yash has been shot on his shoulder, due to which a lot of blood is coming out. Yash's hands and feet are also badly hurt...

###

With great difficulty Yash reaches his home. Asmita sees Yash from the window of his room, Yash is injured. She quickly goes down and bring Yash to his room.

Asmita said, "How did this happen? You should go to the doctor."

"No.... can't go to the doctor." Yash replied.

"Look how much is bleeding...You need treatment as soon as possible." Asmita said.

"I have been shot in the shoulder, take the bullet out of my shoulder."

She gets scared hearing this.

"No wait. a minute. I am not a doctor? I don't do your operation? It will not be going to happen to me."

Yash's wound is very deep and now he has fainted.

Asmita said in nervous voice, "No. No. No. Wait Please Open your eyes...I won't let you die."

And then she runs away and goes to her room and brings first aid kit.

"Open your eyes... please... you don't die now... I'm about to get a bullet out of your shoulder, there will be some pain but please bear it."

Asmita tore the shirt of Yash and then heated the blade and took out the bullet from his shoulder. Then she applies stitches.

###

Next morning, Yash opens his eyes and is surprised to see himself in such condition.... Then Asmita comes to Yash's room, and said, "How are you feeling now?"

"Better....thanks for helping me." Yash replied.

"Well, I didn't want to ask but how did all this happen" Asmita said.

"There are some things which are better if you don't know." Yash replied.

"I will not force you. whenever you want to tell me. My door is always open you can come."

Yash said, "OK"

I have to go now. you take care of yourself. bye." Asmita said.

Yash said, "ok, bye."

Yash's phone rings, Shubham has pulled out all the information about Praneeta's call. Shubham tells Yash over the call.

"Hello, Yash I have sent all the call details of Praneeta on your phone, check it." Shubham said.

"Ok...I'll check. Thanks." Yash replayed.

Yash open the mobile and called last dial number.

Number is ringing but no one is receiving the call. When a call is not received, Yash sends Hallo message to the last dial number. Instant message reply comes. Message is like that...

"Where are you? I was waiting for you., but you didn't come. Meet me today, Hotel Plaza. Room No 502, Night"

And in the reply, Yash will send a message to "OK"

###

A FEW MONTHS BEFORE PRANEETA'S MURDER....

Praneeta 's house (Mumbai) night-The landlord of the room stands outside Praneeta's room and asks for room rent ....

Land lord, "Madam...2 months are done but till now you have not even given full advance of your room... And now you haven't even paid rent. When will I get this rent?"

"I will give you rent in.2...3...days." Praneeta replied.

Land lord, "I have been listening to this word of yours in the last 2 months.... madam these 2. 3.. days don't even come...when will they come...?"

Praneeta said (speaks in anger Voice), "You will get... your... rent."

"God bless me... we should not give room to people like you... I am stuck giving you this room. Madam I have family too. The expenses of my house are met by the rent money."

Praneeta goes to her room.

###

Ladies' beauty parlour, some girls are sitting together & Some are getting facial, some are sitting with haircutting and some face pack.

Kanchan said, "I have got an item song. Make my body fair. What didn't I do to get a chance...?"

Praneeta is also sitting there.

"What did you do...?" Praneeta asked

"This is Bollywood, my sweetheart...whatever is seen here. that's what it for sells" Kanchan replied.

"What did you show?" Praneeta asked.

"Are you new in this line? Slowly you will be learned everything." Kanchan Replied.

"Teach me... I want to learn too." Praneeta said.

Kanchan said, "What's the hurry?"

Kanchan looks at Praneeta's face in the mirror and then Kanchan smokes sitting in the Beauty parlour.

###

Praneeta is shopping in a shopping mall when Nisha's call comes.

Nisha, "Hi. Praneeta, i have an audition update, is a sister's role... will you do this role...?"

"Sister's role?" Praneeta replied.

Nisha said, "Yes"

"What ... what is this? ...you know. I want to be a heroin...and you are giving me the role of sister...?" Praneeta said.

"Listen...you are not a superstar...why are speaking like this, only audition is there, just go and see what happens." Nisha said. If you get selected then do it or else try somewhere else who wants to make you his heroin...

"Ok... you send me the address I will go." Praneeta replied.

"Ok. Bye. Take care."

###

Next day, audition studio, Pranitha stands in front of the camera and speaks her dialogue....

Hi! My name is praneeta, and then she started his dialogue, "I have stumbled so much in life that I don't want to live anymore, there are many people who give sorrow. But there is no one to understand how to live life…"

"Ok…perfect…you will be contacted on phone call…" Camera man said.

"Ok, thanks" Praneeta replied.

###

A few days later Praneeta gets a call from the studio.

"Hello…I am talking to Praneeta?" A girl who spoke on the call.

"Yes. Who are you?" Praneeta replied.

"You auditioned in our studio few days ago and you have been selected …"

"Ok…. good. When is the shooting start?" Praneeta asked.

"You have to come after 2 days… I will send you an address to reach to the studio morning 11am."

And the call gets cut.

###

Praneeta is unable to reach that address due to the high traffic…When she arrives at that address late, her role is given to another girl…. When Praneeta asks to casting team the reason for this, she says that, "you are late, so we have given this role to another girl, now you will not work."

This thing starts hurt to Praneeta's heart and then she comes out from there...

###

Praneeta is going to home sitting in an autorickshaw.... That's when Praneeta gets a phone call ....

Praneeta said, "Hello!"

"Madam your landlord is speaking, I thought I should do a little hello with you. Because you don't even get time to meet us... today 3 days have passed."

"You will get the rent... don't worry." Praneeta replied.

"Madam ji. it's enough now.... You have 07 days' time either give me my rent or you vacate my house...

And she disconnected the call.... She is crying....

###

MAREIN DRIVE- NIGHT

Praneeta is crying on the edge of the sea. She is completely defeated. Giving auditions every day and not getting any work...

She thinks she should go back to Delhi, but she did not run away from Delhi to go back home...

She thinks of her father, about her mother, and about those whom she had left thousands of kilo-meters away...

###

Praneeta is alone in her house. She has completely given up. She cries all night. She smokes and drinks alcohol all night.

###

Praneeta goes to Sunny, and to get work in the film, she starts doing wrong things... Sunny tells Praneeta to sell drugs in the parties. She agrees to do this work. Sunny arranges a meeting with Praneeta, the film producer, politician, business man... During this meeting, he gives money to Praneeta. Many days pass like this.. After working with Sunny, Praneeta has got a lot of money from which she gives the rent of her room to her landlord.

"Here is your complete balance till date." Praneeta said.

"Madam ji Wah.... you have made me very happy today."

"And here is the advance rent of 3 months." Praneeta said.

"Advance of 3months? Madam, where did you get so much money from? Have you robbed a bank?"

"What did you do with this. you got your money...now don't bother me."

###

Praneeta goes to a party. Where she meets a film producer AJJU. He promises to give a lead role in his film.

But before that he asks her to sleep with him. Ajju, "You will play the lead role in my film."

Very loud volume song is playing in the nightclub, due to which Praneeta has to speak a little louder.

"Yes, Off course." Praneeta replied.

Ajju is happy to hear this and on the pretext of saying something to Praneeta, he takes his mouth near her ear.

"You just have to spend a night with me once and I will give you the lead role in my film." Ajju said.

While saying this, he wants to kiss her but Praneeta stops him.

"Hmmm... I give you my number, you call me."

Praneeta leaves after giving her contact number.

###

PRESENT DAY..

The shower of the hotel room is on... Ajju is Taking bath... suddenly someone knock the door of the hotel room badly... If Ajju takes a few seconds more to open the door then the person probably breaks the door because he is very angry...And suddenly he stopped knocking on the door... And when Ajju slowly opened the door, then suddenly he came back.... He would enter the room by pushing Ajju.

"No, you leave me Please, let me go, what do you want? I will give you a lot of money, let me go please." Ajju said.

"You killed my sister, why did she come to see you? And why did you want to meet her in the hotel room." Yash asked.

"She wanted work in the film, it's not that easy to get a work in a film so, she had made a deal with me for his body. And in return I would give her work in my film as a lead role."

"Bastard, do you give work to people in your film by doing this deal? Because of you my sister has lost her life. Are you fond of sleeping with girls? Today I fulfil this hobby of yours. I make you sleep forever." Yash replied.

"No, please let me go, I didn't kill your sister, let me go please. let me go.

Even after many requests, Yash did not have mercy on Ajju and killed him.

###

HOTEL PLAZA–

Police team arrive at the crime scene. ACP Raman Singh said, "send the body for post-mortem, have you got any clues about the murder? Any mark? Who came yesterday to meet him and check all the CCTV cameras of hotels?"

"Sir we checked CCTV but we didn't get anything and yesterday don't disturb tag was put on his door. when the room service person came in the morning, he opened the door with his card and got scared seeing the dead body and informed the manager." SAB INSPECTOR Chetan mane Replied.

"Call him, ask his. Find out with whom was this Ajju yesterday?" ACP Raman Singh said.

"Ok sir" SAB INSPECTOR Chetan mane Replied.

###

POLICE STATION, there is a phone call for ACP Raman Singh at the police station.

SAB INSPECTOR Chetan mane said, "Sir! there's a call for you, He says that all the murders that have happened till now, he has to give information about that. And he will only talk to you."

ACP Raman Singh said, "Hello!

And the sound comes from the phone… "Raman?"

"Yes. Speaking, who are you?" ACP Raman Singh asked.

"Who am I sir don't ask this, why did you do this? I have to know. I just want to live a good life. I don't want to live like you, even you killed people, and no one even knows." The unknown person said on the call.

ACP Raman gets a little scared after listening to him.

"What do you want?" ACP Raman Singh asked.

"Lots of money…and freedom" The unknown person replied.

"Tell me the name who did the murder, and who are you? surrender yourself, Otherwise I will not give you a chance to say anything." ACP Raman Singh replied.

"Well, you're threatening me? And you want to know that what am I doing to you? So, spend as much time as you have to find me. Let me also see whether the policemen ever reach themselves or not." The unknown person replied.

Suddenly call is disconnected.

When calls are disconnected then ACP Raman Singh speaks to SAB-Inspector Chetan MANE for tracing the call.

"Trace this number, and find out where the call came from and who did it?" ACP Raman Singh said.

"Ok sir" SAB INSPECTOR Chetan mane Replied.

###

Yash is sitting alone in the house. Thinking of your sister Praneeta. he Watching the photo of Praneeta.... Yash is missing a lot of her. He has thinking that how his sister has been brutally killed....

###

The police team traces unknown person number that was Rocky's call and goes to his house to arrest him. Seeing the police at his house, Rocky's tries to run away but the police team catches him.

###

ON TV NEWS After 3 days Ajju murder case news on T.V. The killer of Bollywood's famous filmmaker murder case arrested in Hotel Plaza; the police have got success in this case.

The accused whose photo is being shown on TV is of Rocky who was with Praneeta. (As per sunny was said to Yash).

###

POLICE STATION

After arresting Rocky, the police bring him to the station for questioning.

"Tell me, at whose behest did you kill people? And why you killed people." ACP Raman Singh asked.

"I didn't kill anyone." Rocky replied.

"This police station is the only place where people first call themselves innocent. And then after 5 minutes they start telling the whole truth." ACP Raman Singh said.

"I didn't kill anyone." again Rocky replied.

"So why did you call me that day... and why did you say that you know, who did all the murder." ACP Raman Singh asked.

"Yes, I know." Rocky replied.

###

Rocky Sitting on the bus and being taken to the court.... suddenly a car come in very heigh speed... And chase the police van.... And overtaking the police van, the car goes ahead... After some distance, the car comes back in full speed... Police van driver panic in front of car... he loses van control.... the van rolled down in the pit.... then does the black car come in front of the police van ...Yash gets out of his car... All the policemen have been injured. Yash opens the door of the police van, Lifting Rocky on his shoulder, he leaves from that place.

###

Yash takes Rocky to the Under constructed building... Yash removes clothes from Rocky's face. He Beats Rocky very badly....

Chetan mane inform to Raman Singh on call, "Sir Rocky has run away...and the policeman is also injured."

On hearing this, the ACP gets very angry said, "Find out where it is. Chase them... somehow, they couldn't escape, I want him in any condition, bring him Dead or Alive. I don't care. bring his. This is my order. make the blockade everywhere."

"Ok sir" SAB INSPECTOR Chetan mane Replied.

###

A FEW MONTHS BEFORE PRANEETA'S MURDER....

Police raids in the nightclub one day. Many girls are caught in the raid, but no high-profile person is caught. Police ACP Raman Singh find PRANEETA unconscious in a room. ACP Raman Singh takes PRANEETA in his car and takes her to the hospital.

###

When Praneeta one her eyes, she is surprised to see herself in the hospital....

"How did I get to the hospital? And how long have I been here?" Praneeta Asked.

"Madam you were in coma for 6 Months... today you have regained consciousness." ACP Raman Singh said.

Praneeta said, "What? 6 months?"

"Yes"

Praneeta said, "I want to go home."

"Sure... but now there is no point in going home." ACP Raman Singh said.

"What do you mean? There is no point in going home." Praneeta asked.

"I think he has forgotten you, because no one came to meet you. And no one tried to contact you." ACP Raman Singh said.

"I live alone in Mumbai" Praneeta said.

"Doctor, will discharge you shortly. Then I will drop you at your house. ACP Raman Singh said.

###

Raman's car stops at Praneeta's house. He opens the car door, Praneeta comes out of the car....

"Thanks" Praneta said.

As soon as Praneeta goes a little ahead of the car, Raman congratulates her birthday.

"Thanks, but how do you know that today is my birthday?" Praneeta asked.

"I have your ID."

"It means I was unconscious just one day... oh my god you gave shocked." Praneeta replied.

"I even gave a hint in the morning but you probably didn't understand." ACP Raman Singh said.

Praneeta said, "Come on. come to my room. Let's celebrate my birthday.

"Why not, let's go." ACP Raman Singh replied.

Then both go to the room and Praneeta offers a drink to Raman Singh....

After passing a few days in this way the closeness between the two increases and both began to love each other. Raman Singh never told Praneeta that night, nor did Praneeta ever ask. But Raman Singh wanted to save her from the wrong business....

###

Praneeta's phone is ringing....

"Hey...beautiful...how's the mood today??? You are not doing anything these days. .... what happened.... where did that passion of becoming a heroine go?" Sunny said.

"Yes, I remember. I haven't met anyone for just a few days." Praneeta replied.

"You meet me in 30 minutes." Sunny said.

And the call gets disconnected.

###

Praneeta goes to Sunny and Sunny gives her a bag containing a lot of drugs....

"Take this bag and keep it with you and when I tell you, it has to reach a safe place." Sunny said.

"OK" Praneeta replied.

Pranitha takes the bag and hides it in her house....

###

After 3 days Sunny called to Rocky and said, "Go to Praneeta's house. tell her

I gave him the bag, now it's time to bring that bag to the right place."

"Ok" Rocky replied on call.

###

PRESENT DAY.

Yash takes Rocky to the Under constructed building... Yash removes clothes from Rocky's face. Beats Rocky very badly....

Police voice call comes on walkie talkie to CHANETAN MANE...

"Sir, the car whose details were given by you, that car has been found. Right now, he has come and stayed near an under-construction building in Dadar West...maybe there are more people with him." ON DEVICE.

After disconnecting the talkie, Chetan Mane informs ACP Raman Singh.

"Sir his location has been found, just now he has been seen near an under construction building in Dadar West. If you have an order then send a backup tram?"

"Ok" ACP Raman Singh Replied.

###

"Why did you kill Praneeta...? Tell me otherwise I will kill you." Yash asked.

Yash tortures Rocky a lot.

"You will leave me but still he will kill me who killed your sister." Rocky replied.

"Tell me who killed my sister?" Yash asked.

The policemen are surrounding the building from all sides.

"Surround the building from all sides, no one escapes and kills everyone." ACP Raman Singh said.

"Hey... do you think I'm an idiot? Tell me why did you kill my sister?" Yash asked to Rocky.

Rocky laughs loudly...

"HAHAHHHAHAHAHAHAHA! I'm going to die. You think I'll lie to you this time? The ACP who has come. he has not come to catch the murderer. has come to kill. mine and yours.

Yash is furious but he listens to Rocky...

"Why would he kill you...?" Yash asked.

"Because who has done the murder...I only know this thing. And he knows this thing. when he murdered So I made a video. I have saved a copy of it. There is a car outside my house, I have kept it in it, I have a pen drive under the seat. You go from here or else the ACP will kill you too." Rocky said.

Yash jumps out of the window and escapes from that place.

And suddenly police team entered in the room. ACP Raman Singh shot Rocky...1. 2.. 3.. 4..5...6. took off the INTIRE bullets...in his chest.

The police ACP RAMAN SINGH is near Rocky's dead body. After checking the room, the recap just let Sub Inspector CHETAN come in and sent the rest out.

"Tell everyone to stay outside. ACP Raman Singh said.

"Yes Sir" Sab Inspector Chetan Mane replied.

"I want to check this place." ACP Raman Singh Replied.

Then his eyes (ACP Raman Singh) would fall on the photo that fell on the ground, that photo is not of anyone else but of Praneeta. Raman gets shocked seeing this.

###

Yash runs fast and approaches Rocky's car and as he said, take the pen drive from under the seat. And Yash play the video....

Yash played the video... "How dare you interfere in my work?" Praneeta said.

"You promised me that you will not start this work again." ACP Raman Singh said.

"I want work in film, want name. want fame. Which you can't give me." Praneeta Replied.

"So, you will go and spend the night with all of them and get work...?? Will you sell them drugs? ACP Raman Singh asked.

"Yes, I will. Because I want to be a famous movie star. And i will do whatever i have to do for this." Praneeta Replied.

"You B*tch... because of girls like you all people are infamous.

ACP Raman Singh starts throttling Praneeta's throat while speaking...and doesn't leave till she dies...

Sunny had sent Rocky to get the bag... but after hearing the sound coming from the room, he stopped and took to record the video in his mobile.

Police goes to Rocky's house to search...

That's when Yash sees him... As soon as Yash's eyes fall on Raman, he pounces on him like a dreaded Animal....There is a lot of fight between both of them... and between the two, Sub Inspector Chetan also gets shot on the shoulder...After a long fight, Yash shoots Raman with his gun. Yash runs away and he take Praneeta's photo from Raman's pocket.

###

Praneeta's mother and father are watching news on TV and they both got emotional.

On News Channel, "The murderer of the Mumbai massacre was killed in an encounter with the police last night. And in tease ACP Raman Singh lost his life... And Sub Inspector Chetan will be given gallantry medal. A video recording has also been found in Chatan in which ACP Raman had murdered a girl named Praneeta a few days back... Who left her home and family from Delhi and came to Mumbai to fulfil her dream?"

###

MARRINE DRIVE – SUNSET EVENING-

Yash is sitting with Asmita and sees his sister's PRANEETA'S photo. After Seeing YASH condition, ASHMITA understands what would have happened that night....and then both hug and Kiss....

*********THE END**********